# THIS IS A
# MOOSE

This
is the
Mighty
Moose.

His father
is a moose.

His mother
is a moose.

This moose wants to be an astronaut.

This is a moose - Take Two!
THIS IS A MOOSE
DIR.: BILLY WADDLER
E 2
SCENE: MOOSE INTRODUCTION
CAM.: CHIP N. ZEE

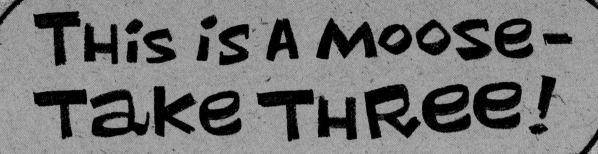

Grandmother Moose
and Regal Giraffe

prepare to launch
Mighty Moose into space.

What just happened?

The moose has been launched.

Look at that moose go!

Actually, I'm a chipmunk.

I'M COMING, ASTROMOOSE!!!

The end

# Glossary of Filmmaking Terms

**BOOM MICROPHONE:** A long pole with a microphone on the end. If you're recording a giraffe, a very long pole is recommended.

**CAMERA OPERATOR:** A monkey who controls the camera.

**CLAPPER:** A small board with a hinge that you "clap" to start each take. Watch your paws!

**CUT:** A term said by the director to end the take. Often used in frustration, as in, "Cut. Cut! *Cut!!!*"

**DIRECTOR:** A duck in charge of making the movie. Unless, of course, you're filming a moose who wants to be an astronaut.

**GAFFER:** A bear responsible for lighting the set—always happy to be paid in honey.

**MEGAPHONE:** A large cone used for making your voice louder. Useful for a director with a moose problem.

**ROCKET-POWERED CANOE:** *—"Cut!"*

**SET:** The location where the filming of the movie takes place, either on Earth or on the moon.

**TAKE:** A single recording of a scene. The more things go wrong, the more takes there are!

For Alice

*—Richard T. Morris*

To my dad, the most influential artist in my life

*—Tom Lichtenheld*

**About This Book**

This book was edited by Connie Hsu and designed by Tom Lichtenheld and Steve Scott with art direction by Patti Ann Harris. The production was supervised by Erika Schwartz, and the production editor was Christine Ma. The type is Stymie and hand-lettering. The illustrations were rendered in ink, colored pencil, and gouache on Mi-Teintes paper, with digital enhancement by Kristen Cella.

ISBN 978-0-545-88275-0 • Text copyright © 2014 by Richard T. Morris. Illustrations copyright © 2014 by Tom Lichtenheld. All rights reserved. Published by Scholastic Inc., 557 Broadway, New York, NY 10012, by arrangement with Little, Brown Books for Young Readers, a division of Hachette Book Group, Inc. SCHOLASTIC and associated logos are trademarks and/or registered trademarks of Scholastic Inc.

12 11 10 9 8 7 6 5 4 3 2 1        15 16 17 18 19 20/0 • Printed in the U.S.A.        40 • First Scholastic printing, September 2015

STBY

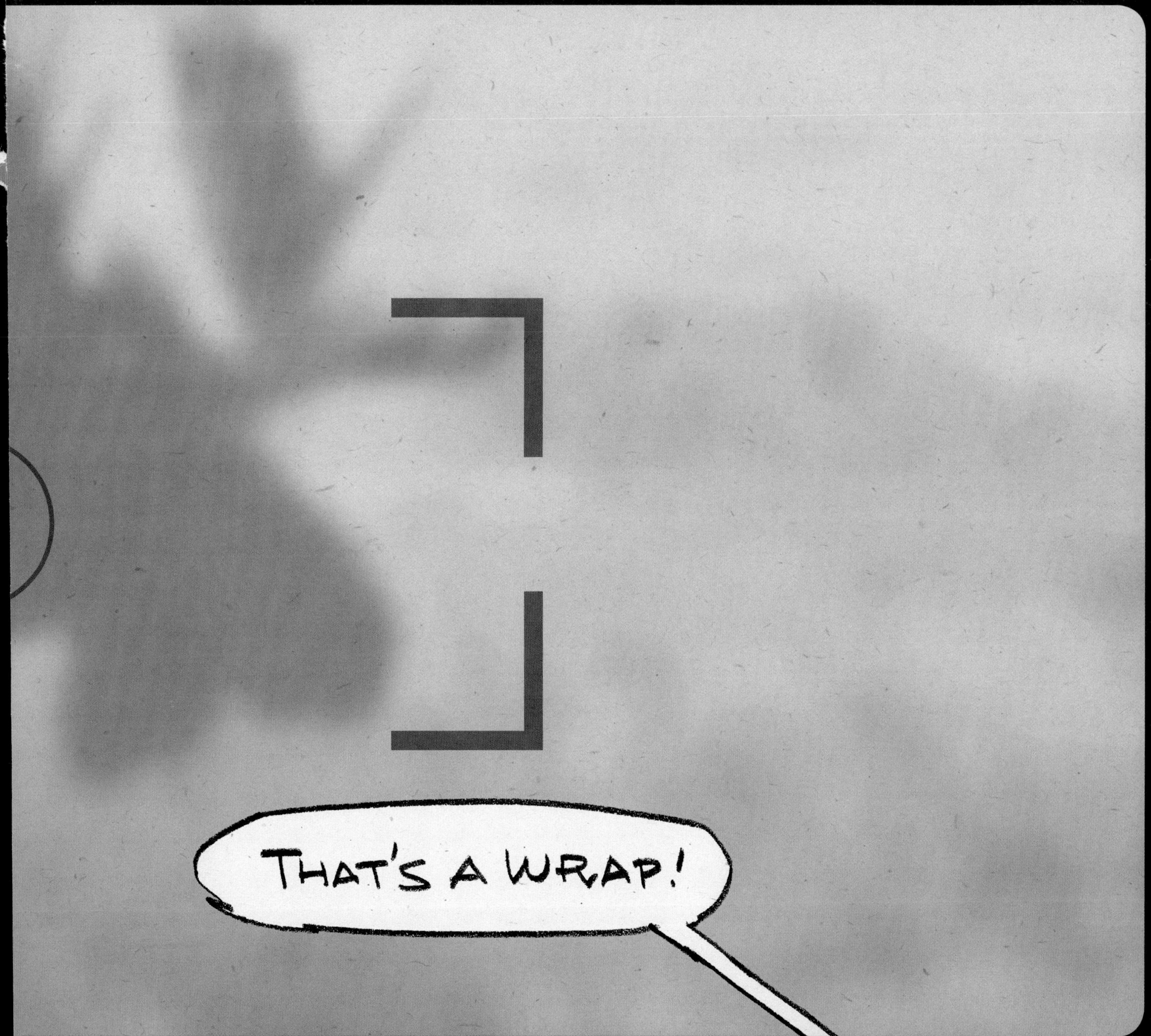
THAT'S A WRAP!